NOT SUPERWOMAN

Written & created by
Emma Dennis-Edwards

Directed & created by
Lynette Linton

|| SAMUEL FRENCH ||

USE OF COPYRIGHTED MUSIC

A licence issued by Concord Theatricals to perform this play does not include permission to use the incidental music specified in this publication. In the United Kingdom: Where the place of performance is already licensed by the PERFORMING RIGHT SOCIETY (PRS) a return of the music used must be made to them. If the place of performance is not so licensed then application should be made to PRS for Music (www.prsformusic.com). A separate and additional licence from PHONOGRAPHIC PERFORMANCE LTD (www.ppluk.com) may be needed whenever commercial recordings are used. Outside the United Kingdom: Please contact the appropriate music licensing authority in your territory for the rights to any incidental music.

USE OF COPYRIGHTED THIRD-PARTY MATERIALS

Licensees are solely responsible for obtaining formal written permission from copyright owners to use copyrighted third-party materials (e.g., artworks, logos) in the performance of this play and are strongly cautioned to do so. If no such permission is obtained by the licensee, then the licensee must use only original materials that the licensee owns and controls. Licensees are solely responsible and liable for clearances of all third-party copyrighted materials, and shall indemnify the copyright owners of the play(s) and their licensing agent, Concord Theatricals Ltd., against any costs, expenses, losses and liabilities arising from the use of such copyrighted third-party materials by licensees.

IMPORTANT BILLING AND CREDIT REQUIREMENTS

If you have obtained performance rights to this title, please refer to your licensing agreement for important billing and credit requirements.

NOTE

This edition reflects a rehearsal draft of the script and may differ from the final production.

NOT YOUR SUPERWOMAN was originally produced by Bush Theatre with support from Charles Holloway OBE, Eleanor Lloyd Productions and Eilene Davidson Productions, and premiered in the Holloway Theatre on 6 September 2025. The cast and creative team were as follows:

JOYCE . . . . Golda Rosheuvel
ERICA . . . . .Letitia Wright

Writer & Creator . . . . Emma Dennis-Edwards
Director & Creator. . . . . Lynette Linton
Set & Costume Designer . . . . Alex Berry
Lighting Designer . . . . .Jai Morjaria
Video Designer. . . . . .Gino Ricardo Green
Sound Designer . . . . Max Pappenheim
Composer . . . . .XANA
Movement Director . . . . Shelley Maxwell
Hair & Makeup Designer . . . . .Cynthia De La Rosa
Dramaturg. . . . . Deirdre O'Halloran
Production Dramatherapy . . . . Wabriya King
Costume Supervisor . . . . .Esther Taylor
Voice & Accent Coach . . . . .Hazel Holder
Assistant Director . . . . .Amelia Michaels
Lighting Programmer . . . . .Luca Panetta
Associate Video Designer . . . . Daberichi Ukoha-Kalu

Production Manager . . . . .Chloe Stally-Gibson
Company Stage Manager . . . . .Anna Sheard
Assistant Stage Manager . . . . .Africa Blagrove

Set Builder . . . . .Centreline Fabrications
Production Electrician . . . . Kevin James
Production Sound Engineer. . . . . .Sasha Howe
Video Engineer. . . . . Ieuan Watkins-Hyde

For Bush Theatre:
Lead Producer . . . . Nikita Karia
Associate Director . . . . .Katie Greenall
Press Manager . . . . Martin Shippen
Marketing Campaign Lead . . . . Kelly Thurston
Technical & Building Manager . . . . Jamie Haigh
Production Technician . . . . .Harry Faulkner

With special thanks to Daniel Bailey, Leon Belony, Courtney Phillip, Doug Kerr, Emma McRae, Harvey Araja, Toyin Dawudu and Mahlon Prince.

CAST

GOLDA ROSHEUVEL | Joyce

Golda Rosheuvel is a well-revered British actress best known for her stage work and more recently her role as Queen Charlotte in the hit Netflix series *Bridgerton*. Created by Shonda Rhimes, it is one of the most successful shows Netflix has produced. The limited spin-off series *Queen Charlotte: A Bridgerton Story* chronicling the young queen also launched to critical and commercial success in 2023.

Previously she starred in the hugely successful sci-fi epic *Dune*, directed by Denis Villeneuve. Other film credits include *Lady Macbeth*, *I Remember You*, *Coma Girl*, and *Lava*. Her television work includes *Silent Witness*, *A Confessions*, *Luther* and *Death in Paradise*.

A veteran of the stage, Golda has starred in a number of critically acclaimed theatre productions including: *Othello*, *A Christmas Carol*, *Electra*, *Carmen Jones* (The Old Vic); *We Will Rock You* (Dominion Theatre); *The Tempest*, *Julius Caesar* and *Antony and Cleopatra* (RSC West End).

In 2024 Golda starred in Pixar animation *Orion and the Dark* and appeared in the new series *Doctor Who*. She will next be seen in *Bridgerton Season 4*, Colin Tilly's debut film *Somewhere in Dreamland* before leading the cast in Sky Original film *Grow*.

LETITIA WRIGHT | Erica

Letitia Wright is an award winning Guyanese-British actor, producer, writer and director. In 2018, she attained global recognition and critical acclaim for her portrayal of Princess Shuri in Marvel Studios' *Black Panther*, assuming the titular role in the 2022 sequel *Black Panther: Wakanda Forever* – the highest grossing female-led superhero film in the history of the United States box office.

Along with 3.16 Productions and roles in recent art-house projects; the critically acclaimed Ireland-set drama *Aisha* and her BIFA award winning turn in *The Silent Twins*, Wright has cemented her position as one of the industry's most captivating young artists both in front of and behind the camera.

2025 sees Letitia make her directorial debut with *Highway To The Moon*, a moving coming-of-age fantasy drama which follows the experiences of young black men whose lives have been abruptly snatched away, before her long-awaited return to the stage in *Not Your Superwoman* at the Bush Theatre. Next year, Wright will make her National Theatre debut in *The Story*, before returning to the MCU to reprise her role as Black Panther in *Avengers: Doomsday*.

Past credits include: *The Convert* at Young Vic Theatre, Steve McQueen's *Small Axe*, Dominic Savage's *I Am*, *Urban Hymn*, *Guava Island*, *Humans*, *Cucumber*, *My Brother the Devil*, *Top Boy* and the critically acclaimed sci-fi series *Black Mirror*, which earned her an Emmy nomination for 'Outstanding Supporting Actress in a Limited Series or Movie'.

CREATIVE

EMMA DENNIS-EDWARDS | Writer & Creator

Emma Dennis-Edwards is a writer and performer of Jamaican and Trinidadian heritage whose work spans theatre and television. Her acclaimed solo play *Funeral Flowers* premiered at the Edinburgh Fringe Festival, winning a Scotsman Fringe First Award and the Filipa Bragança Award for Best Female Solo Performance. The production toured London to critical acclaim. Her play *Bricks* was developed through the Old Vic 12 programme and shortlisted for the Alfred Fagon Award. Emma is currently under commission with Cardboard Citizens and Clean Break, continuing her commitment to socially driven storytelling.

On screen, her original drama *Consent* aired on Channel 4 and was nominated for both Broadcast and RTS Awards, with Emma nominated for Best Writer – Drama at the RTS Awards. She has also written for BBC series including *Champion*, *Boarders*, *EastEnders*, *Holby City*, and *Casualty*.

LYNETTE LINTON | Director & Creator

Lynette Linton is a writer and BAFTA-nominated director for theatre, television and film, and is the outgoing Artistic Director of the Bush Theatre. Recent work as a Director includes *Intimate Apparel* (Donmar Warehouse); *Alterations* (National Theatre); *Barcelona* (The Duke of York's Theatre) and *Shifters* (Bush Theatre/The Duke of York's Theatre). She returns to the Bush Theatre to direct *Not Your Superwoman* followed by the world premiere of *The Boy Who Harnessed the Wind* with the Royal Shakespeare Company.

She ran the Bush Theatre from 2019-2025 during which her programming centred on ground-breaking debuts from UK and Irish writers. It saw four consecutive Olivier Award wins for Richard Gadd's *Baby Reindeer*, Igor Memic's *Old Bridge*, Waleed Akhtar's *The P Word* and Matilda Feyiṣayọ Ibini's *Sleepova*, plus the West End transfers of both Tyrell Williams' *Red Pitch* and Benedict Lombe's *Shifters* in 2024.

She was previously Resident Assistant Director at the Donmar Warehouse and is a co-founder of production company Black Apron Entertainment.

Credits include: *Intimate Apparel, Clyde's* (Donmar Warehouse); *Alterations, Blues for an Alabama Sky* – Evening Standard Theatre Award for Best Director and Critics' Circle Award for Best Director (National Theatre); *Barcelona* (The Duke of York's Theatre); *Shifters* (Bush Theatre/The Duke of York's Theatre); *As We Face The Sun* – as co-director with Katie Greenall, *August in England* – as co-director with Daniel Bailey, *House Of Ife, Chiaroscuro* (Bush Theatre); *Sweat* – Black British Theatre Award for Best Director (Donmar Warehouse/Gielgud Theatre); *Richard II* – co-directed with Adjoa Andoh, marking the first ever company of women of colour in a Shakespeare play on a major UK stage (Shakespeare's Globe); *Assata Taught Me* (Gate Theatre); *Function* (National Youth Theatre).

Television credits include: *My Name is Leon* (BAFTA nomination for Emerging Talent: Fiction).

ALEX BERRY | Set & Costume Designer

Alex Berry is a set and costume designer for theatre, opera and film based in London. She trained at Bristol Old Vic Theatre School having previously studied at the Royal Northern College of Music and Koninklijk Conservatorium, The Netherlands, as a musician. She was recently nominated for best costume design for *Macbeth (an undoing)* in the Drama Desk Awards 2024, New York.

Recent projects include: *Intimate Apparel* (Donmar Warehouse); *Shifters* (Bush Theatre/The Duke of York's Theatre); *Treasure Island, Macbeth (an undoing)* (Lyceum, Edinburgh); *Hansël Und Gretel* (Royal Academy of Music); *Trials and Passions of Unfamous Women* (Clean Break, Brixton House); *Every Brilliant Thing* (Theatre by the Lake); *A Matter of Choice* (Panoptic Films); *The Barber of Seville, Don Giovanni* (Nevill Holt Opera); *No Sweat* (The Pleasance Theatre); *The Rape of Lucretia* (Royal Conservatoire of Scotland); *Spring Awakening* (Redgrave Theatre); *Right Place Wrong Tim* (Channel 4); *A Tender Thing* (The Theatre, Chipping Norton); *Rabbits* (Park Theatre); *The Cunning Little Vixen* (Royal College of Music); *The Lighthouse* (Hackney Showroom); *Song of Riots* (Battersea Arts Centre); *The River* (Brewery); *Blue Stockings* (Tobacco Factory).

JAI MORJARIA | Lighting Designer

Jai trained at RADA.

Theatre design includes: *Intimate Apparel, The Trials* (Donmar Warehouse); *Barcelona* (The Duke of York's Theatre); *Why Am I So Single?* (Garrick Theatre); *Othello* (National Theatre); *The Buddha of Suburbia* (RSC); *The Secret Garden* (Regent's Park Open Air Theatre); *Wuthering Heights* (National/International Tour); *Animal Farm* (Stratford East/ Leeds Playhouse); *Choir* (Chichester Festical Theatre); *Abigail's Party*

(Royal Exchange); *Barnum* (Watermill); *Macbeth* (International Tour/Shakespeare Theatre Company, Washington); *Cuckoo* (Royal Court Theatre); *Accidental Death of an Anarchist* (Haymarket/Lyric Hammersmith/Sheffield); *My Son's A Queer (But What Can You Do?)* (New York City Center/Ambassadors/Garrick/Turbine); *August in England, House of Ife, Lava* (Bush Theatre); *Chasing Hares* (Young Vic); *Lost and Found* (Factory International); *I'll Take You To Mrs. Cole* (Complicité).

Film design includes: *The Magic Finger* (Roald Dahl Company).

Awards include Association of Lighting Designer's ETC Award; nominated for Helen Hayes Award for Outstanding Lighting Design and Honourable Mention for Profile Award for Theatre Lighting.

GINO RICARDO GREEN | Video Designer

Gino Ricardo Green is a director and video/projection designer. He is the co-founder of Black Apron Entertainment.

Credits as Video/Projection Designer include: *Backstroke, Intimate Apparel* (Donmar Warehouse); *Barcelona, Treason: The Musical in Concert* (West End); *A Child of Science* (Bristol Old Vic); *Samuel Takes A Break, The Flea* (The Yard Theatre); *The Legends Of Them* (Hackney Showroom/Brixton House); *I* (ATC/Stratford East/UK Tour); *Wolves on Road, August in England, Lava* (Bush Theatre); *Othello* (National, as Co-Video Designer); *The Ballad of St Johns Carpark* (Icon); *That is Not Who I Am* (Royal Court Theatre); *Kabul Goes Pop: Music Television Afghanistan* (Brixton House/Hightide); *Edge* (NYT); *Children's Children* (ETT, as Director of Photography/Editor); *Beyond The Canon and Poor Connection* (RADA); *Sweat* (Donmar Warehouse/West End); *Passages: A Windrush Celebration* (Black Apron at the Royal Court Theatre); *Hashtag Lightie* (Arcola Theatre); *Lightie* (The Gate Theatre).

Credits as Associate include: *Small Island* (National Theatre); *Get Up Stand Up! The Bob Marley Musical* (West End); *Be More Chill* (The Other Palace & West End).

MAX PAPPENHEIM | Sound Designer

Theatre includes: *The Night of the Iguana, Cruise* (West End); *The Children* (Broadway); *Noughts and Crosses, Twelfth Night* (Regent's Park Open Air Theatre); *A Raisin in the Sun* (Headlong); *The Forsyte Saga* (Park Theatre); *Henry V* (Globe); *The School for Scandal, Crooked Dances* (RSC); *Coram Boy, Macbeth* (Chichester Festival Theatre); *Shed: Exploded View* (Royal Exchange); *A Doll's House Part 2, The Way of the World* (Donmar Warehouse); *The Habits, The Invention of Love, Blackout Songs, Labyrinth* (Hampstead Theatre); *Feeling Afraid, Old Bridge* (Bush Theatre); *Creditors, Blue/Heart, The Distance* (Orange Tree

Theatre); *The Talented Mr Ripley, Picture You Dead, The Mirror Crack'd* (National tours); *Ophelias Zimmer* (Schaubühne/Royal Court Theatre).

Opera and Ballet includes: *The Limit* (Royal Ballet); *Miranda* (Opéra Comique, Paris); *Scraww* (Trebah Gardens). Associate Artist of Orange Tree Theatre, The Faction and Silent Opera. Awards include Off West End Award for Sound Design for *Old Bridge*.

XANA | Composer

Xana is a composer, spatial sound artist and a haptic specialist sound designer developing accessible audio systems for theatre.

Theatre credits: *After Sunday* (Belgrade Theatre); *Alterations* (National Theatre); *Speed, The Real Ones, My Father's Fable, Elephant, Sleepova, The P Word, Strange Fruit* and *Shifters* (Bush Theatre); *The Architect* (ATC/GDIF); *Pig Heart Boy* (Unicorn); *Barcelona* (Duke of York's Theatre); *Beautiful Thing* (Stratford East); *Imposter 22, Word:Play, Living Newspaper #4* (Royal Court Theatre); *Rumble In the Jungle* (Rematch:Live); *Intimate Apparel, The Trials, Marys Seacole* (Donmar Warehouse); *Anna Karerina* (Edinburgh Lyceum/Bristol Old Vic); *Sundown Kiki, Earthworks, Sundown Kiki Reloaded, The Collaboration, Changing Destiny, Fairview, Ivan and the Dogs* (Young Vic); *Burgerz* (Hackney Showroom); *King Troll [The Fawn], Everyday (Deafinitely)* (New Diorama Theatre); *Blood Knot, Guards At The Taj* (Orange Tree); *Samuel Takes A Break* (Yard).

Awards include: BBTA Award-winner for Best Sound Design 2023 and 2024; Offie Award-winner for *King Troll, Shifters* and *Guards at the Taj*; Offie Award nominations for *Sleepova, The P Word* and *Blood Knot*; Olivier Affiliate Production award for *The P Word* and *Sleepova*.

SHELLEY MAXWELL | Movement Director

Shelley Maxwell won the award for Best Choreographer at the inaugural Black British Theatre Awards in 2019 for her work on *Equus*.

Theatre includes: *Macbeth* (Donmar Warehouse); *The Time Traveller's Wife* (Apollo Theatre); *Mlima's Tale* (Kiln); *Untitled F*ck M*ss S**gon Play* (Royal Exchange/Young Vic); *August in England* (Bush Theatre); *The Secret Life of Bees* (Almeida Theatre); *Best of Enemies* (Noël Coward Theatre/Young Vic); *Tartuffe* (Birmingham Rep); *The Time Traveller's Wife: The Musical* (Storyhouse); *Get Up, Stand Up! The Bob Marley Story* (Lyric); *J'Ouvert* (Harold Pinter Theatre/Theatre503); *After Life, Master Harold...and the Boys, Hansard, Antony and Cleopatra, Twelfth Night* (National Theatre); *Nine Night* (National Theatre/Trafalgar Theatre); *Equus* (Stratford East/Trafalgar Theatre); *Tartuffe* (RSC); *Macbeth* (Shakespeare's Globe); *Faustus* (Headlong at Lyric/Birmingham Rep); *Cinderella* (Lyric); *Grey* (Ovalhouse); *King Hedley II* (Stratford East);

Cougar, Dealing with Clair (Orange Tree); *Winter, Why It's Kicking off Everywhere* (Young Vic); *Cuttin' It* (Young Vic/Royal Court Theatre); *A Streetcar Named Desire* (Nuffield/Clwyd Theatre Cymru/English Touring Theatre); *Rules for Living* (Royal & Derngate Theatre/Rose Theatre/English Touring Theatre); *Apologia* (English Theatre Frankfurt).

Television/Film includes: *The Marvels* (Disney); *Anansi Boys* (upcoming on Amazon); *Ear for Eye* (BBC/Fruit Tree Media); *Romeo & Juliet* (Sky Arts/PBS/National Theatre).

CYNTHIA DE LA ROSA | Hair and Makeup Designer

Cynthia De La Rosa's design in theatre includes: *Alterations, Blues for an Alabama Sky, Standing at the Sky's Edge, Beginning* (National Theatre); *Slave Play, Beginning, Barcelona, Shifters, Standing at the Sky's Edge* (West End); *"Daddy": A Melodrama, The Tragedy of Macbeth, Shipwreck, The Twilight Zone, Against and Boy* (Almeida Theatre); *Jitney, Sylvia* (Old Vic); *The Watsons* (Menier Chocolate Factory); *Allelujah!* (Bridge Theatre); *Strange Fruit, Boys Will Be Boys* (Bush Theatre); *Frost/Nixon* (Sheffield Crucible); *The Convert, A Midsummer Night's Dream, Once in a Lifetime* (Young Vic); *Clyde's, Intimate Apparel* (Donmar Warehouse).

TV Design includes: *Too Much, We Are Lady Parts, Everyone Else Burns, Dreaming Whilst Black, Stath Lets Flats, Riches.* Film Design includes: *Animol*, and short films *Tommies, My Jerome, I Am Mary, The Track, Farewell She Goes.*

DEIRDRE O'HALLORAN | Dramaturg

Deirdre O'Halloran is a dramaturg specialising in the development of new plays and musicals. Deirdre is the Head of New Musical Theatre at Birmingham Hippodrome, the first department of its kind in the UK where she is developing new musicals of all scales. She was previously Literary Manager at the Bush Theatre, where she designed artist development programmes, and dramaturged all commissioned work.

Highlights of her produced work include: Edinburgh Fringe 2025 hit musical *Hot Mess* by Jack Godfrey and Ellie Coote, *Shifters* by Benedict Lombe (Duke of York's Theatre); winner of the Evening Standard Award *Red Pitch* by Tyrell Williams (@SohoPlace); *August in England* by Lenny Henry, the Olivier award-winning plays *The P Word* by Waleed Akhtar and *Sleepova* by Matilda Feyişayọ Ibini.

As a freelancer, Deirdre has worked with many leading producers and theatres, including Eleanor Lloyd Productions, Regent's Park Open Air Theatre, DEM Productions and Paines Plough.

WABRIYA KING | Production Dramatherapy

Wabriya is the Associate Dramatherapist for the Bush Theatre and has supported all productions since 2021

Recent Theatre credits include: *Intimate Apparel, Clyde's* (Donmar Warehouse); *Alterations, Blues for an Alabama Sky* (National Theatre); *Elektra, Barcelona, Shifters* (Duke of York's Theatre); *Slave Play* (Noël Coward Theatre); *Otherland, Roots, Look Back in Anger* (Almeida Theatre); *Tambo & Bones, Now, I See* (Stratford East); *Wicked, Cabaret, Hamilton, Moulin Rouge, MJ The Musical* (West End).

Film: *The Changing Room* (Anima Goli Productions); *Empire of Light* (Searchlight Pictures); *Chevalier* (Element Pictures).

ESTHER TAYLOR | Costume Supervisor

Esther is a Fashion Stylist working on commercial and editorial projects. She studied Textile for Fashion Design at Manchester School of Art and has worked for brands like Getty Images, Nike, John Lewis, Jack Wills and ASOS. She is excited to join the world of costume for the first time for *Not Your Superwoman* at the Bush.

HAZEL HOLDER | Voice & Accent Coach

Theatre includes: *Alterations, The Importance of Being Earnest, A Tupperware of Ashes, The Hot Wing King, Death of England trilogy, The Effect, Grenfell: in the words of survivors, Small Island, Nine Night, Barber Shop Chronicles, Angels in America* (National Theatre); *Clyde's, A Doll's House, Part 2, Marys Seacole, Constellations* (Donmar Warehouse); *The Seagull* (Barbican); *Stereophonic, Waiting for Godot, Sunset Blvd., The Glass Menagerie, 2:22, C*ck, Tina: The Tina Turner Musical, Dreamgirls* (resident director) (West End), *Ulster American* (Riverside Studios); *Mlima's Tale, Retrograde, Pass Over* (Kiln); *The Homecoming, Best of Enemies, Death of a Salesman, The Convert* (Young Vic); *Giant, ear for eye, Pigs and Dogs* (Royal Court Theatre); *August in England* (Bush Theatre); *Richard II* (Sam Wanamaker Playhouse).

Television includes: *A Thousand Blows* (Disney +); *Silo* (Apple TV+); *Small Axe* (BBC). Film includes: *The Ministry of Ungentlemanly Warfare* (Amazon); *The Silent Twins* (Focus Features).

AMELIA MICHAELS | Assistant Director

Amelia Michaels is a British-Bajan Actor, Director, TheatreMaker and Facilitator born and bred between London and the Midlands. She is a hybrid in many aspects which has been her superpower, allowing her to work across various forms, disciplines and communities. In 2024 and 2025, she solo produced seven shows across five festivals of her debut play *MANDEM* for which she is also the Writer and Co-Director. An alumnus of China Plate's well established producing course 'Optimists', Amelia is currently focusing on birthing her directing career. Outside of her own work she's most recently assisted Corey Campbell on *Romeo & Juliet* (a Belgrade Theatre, Bristol Old Vic and Hackney Empire co-production). She's currently a member of the 2025/26 'New Associates' cohort with New Perspectives Theatre company in order to support the overall growth of her practice, and as an actor she can most recently be seen in *Suspect* on Disney+.

LUCA PANETTA | Lighting Programmer

Luca is a freelance Lighting Designer, Associate, and Lighting Programmer. He trained at LAMDA (London Academy of Music & Dramatic Arts) in Production Technical Arts.

As LX Programmer, Luca has worked on shows at venues such as Donmar Warehouse, Young Vic, Watermill Theatre, Chichester, NTLive & Bush Theatre, and across the West End

Credits as Associate include: *Barcelona*, *Why Am I So Single* (West End); *Macbeth* (2023/24 UK WarehouseTour); *The Merchant of Venice 1936* (RSC & UK Tour); *A Face In The Crowd* (Young Vic); A Playlist for the Revolution (Bush).

Credits as Lighting Designer include: *Maria de Rudenz* (Battersea Arts Centre) for which he won a Profile award for Outstanding Achievement in Opera; *Edith* (The Lowry/Theatr Clwyd); If Opera's 2022, 2023, 2025 Seasons; *Diary of a Somebody* (Seven Dials Playhouse) for which he was nominated for an Offie in Lighting Design; *Polko* (Paines Plough Roundabout).

DABERECHI UKOHA-KALU | Associate Video Designer

Daberechi Ukoha-Kalu is a multidisciplinary artist whose practice is rooted in storytelling and performance. She uses her technical skills to build new worlds across theatre and installation art.

Theatre credits as Video Programmer includes: *Intimate Apparel*, *Backstroke*, *Fear of 13* (Donmar Warehouse); *Ruination* (Royal Opera House); *Barcelona* (Duke of York's Theatre); *Mean Girls* (Savoy Theatre); *Othello* (National Theatre); *Oklahoma!* (Young Vic).

Theatre credits as Video Designer includes: *Whose Planet Are You On?* (Old Vic); *Up Close* (Menier).

Other theatre credits includes: *The Band's Visit* (Donmar Warehouse); *King Lear* (Wyndham's); *Violet Disruption* (Finnish National Opera); Guardians of The Galaxy Secret Cinema.

Concert credits as Lighting and Video Designer includes: *Pink Pantheress* (Camp Flog Gnaw) and *George Riley* (Headline show).

CHLOE STALLY-GIBSON | Production Manager

Chloe is a freelance production manager and former associate artist of Zoo Co Theatre Company and ChewBoy Productions.

Her recent work includes: *Shifters* (Bush Theatre & Duke of York's Theatre); *Punch, A Face In The Crowd* (Young Vic); *Perfect Show For Rachel* (Barbican); *Tender, This Might Not Be It, Insane Asylum Seekers* (Bush Theatre); *Playhouse Creatures* (JCTP); *Silence* (Tara Theatre).

ANNA SHEARD | Company Stage Manager

Anna trained at the Royal Welsh College of Music and Drama.

Credits for Bush Theatre include: *Chiasoscuro*

Credits for other theatre include: *Intimate Apparel, Clyde's, Teenage Dick, Sweat* (Donmar); *Alterations, Blues for an Alabama Sky* (National Theatre); *The School for Scandal* (RSC); *An Enemy of the People* (Wessex Grove, Duke of York's Theatre); *Barcelona* (ATG, Duke of York's Theatre); *Pressure* (Royal Alexandra Theatre, Toronto, Jonathan Church Ltd); *Romeo and Juliet* (Shakespeare's Globe); *The Vortex, Crave, random/ generations* (Chichester Festival Theatre); *The Fellowship, Peggy for You* (Hampstead Theatre); *After the End* (Stratford East); *House/Amongst the Reeds* (Clean Break); *Trust, Twilight: Los Angeles 1992, Assata Taught Me, I Call My Brothers* (Gate Theatre).

AFRICA BLAGROVE | Assistant Stage Manager

Africa Blagrove is an Assistant Stage Manager based in London with Jamaican heritage. She began her stage management journey after securing a work placement with *Get Up! Stand Up! The Bob Marley Musical*, which sparked her passion for the stage management industry.

Africa has a deep passion for creating and sourcing props that help bring theatre to life. They find joy in the details and discovering or crafting pieces that enhance storytelling, reveal character, and ground the world of the play in something tangible.

Her ASM credits include: *1536* (Almeida Theatre); *Play On!* (Bristol Old Vic & Lyric Hammersmith); *Alice in Wonderland* (Brixton House); *My Father's Fable* (Bush Theatre); *Samuel Takes a Break ...* (Yard); *#Blackis...* (New Diorama Theatre).

Bush Theatre

We make theatre for London. Now.

For over 50 years the Bush Theatre has been a world-famous home for new plays and an internationally renowned champion of playwrights.

Combining ambitious artistic programming with meaningful community engagement work and industry leading talent development schemes, the Bush Theatre champions and supports unheard voices to develop the artists and audiences of the future.

Since opening in 1972 the Bush has produced more than 500 ground-breaking premieres of new plays, developing an enviable reputation for its acclaimed productions nationally and internationally.

They have nurtured the careers of writers including James Graham, Lucy Kirkwood, Temi Wilkey, Jonathan Harvey and Jack Thorne. Recent successes include Tyrell Williams' *Red Pitch*, Benedict Lombe's *Shifters*, and Arinzé Kene's *Misty*. The Bush has won over 100 awards including the Olivier Award for Outstanding Achievement in Affliate Theatre for the past four years for Richard Gadd's *Baby Reindeer*, Igor Memic's *Old Bridge*, Waleed Akhtar's *The P Word* and Matilda Feyiṣayọ Ibini's *Sleepova*.

Located in the renovated old library on Uxbridge Road in the heart of Shepherd's Bush, the Bush Theatre continues to create a space where all communities can be part of its future and call the theatre home.

'The place to go for ground-breaking work as diverse as its audiences' EVENING STANDARD

bushtheatre.co.uk
@bushtheatre

h&f
hammersmith & fulham

ARTS COUNCIL
ENGLAND

Supported by
ARTS COUNCIL
ENGLAND

THANK YOU

Our supporters make our work possible. Together, we're evolving the canon and creating a bolder, more diverse, and representative future for British theatre. We're so grateful to you all.

MAJOR DONORS
Charles Holloway OBE
Jim & Michelle Gibson
Georgia Oetker
Cathy & Tim Score
Susie Simkins
Jack Thorne
Gianni & Michael Alen-Buckley

SHOOTING STARS
Jim & Michelle Gibson
Anthony Marraccino & Mariela Manso
Cathy & Tim Score
Susie Simkins

LONE STARS
Clyde Cooper
Adam Kenwright
Jim Marshall

HANDFUL OF STARS
Charlie Bigham
Judy Bollinger
Richard & Sarah Clarke
Christopher delaMare
Sue Fletcher
Thea Guest
Kate Hamer Ltd.
Elizabeth Jack
Simon & Katherine Johnson
Garry & Lorna Lawrence
Phyllida Lloyd & Kate Pakenham
Vivienne Lukey
Sam & Jim Murgatroyd
Georgia Oetker
Mark & Anne Paterson
Miguel & Valeri Ramos Handal

Bhagat Sharma
Dame Emma Thompson
Joe Tinston & Amelia Knott

RISING STARS
Elizabeth Beebe
Martin Blackburn
David Brooks
Catharine Browne
Anthony Chantry
Lauren Clancy
Caroline Clasen
Susan Cuff
Matthew Cushen
Anne-Hélène and Rafaël Biosse Duplan
Austin Erwin
Kim Evans
Mimi Findlay
Jack Gordon
Hugh & Sarah Grootenhuis
Uzma Hasan
Lesley Hill & Russ Shaw
Davina & Malcolm Judelson
Joanna Kennedy
Mike Lewis
Lynette Linton
Tim & Deborah Maunder
Michael McCoy
Judy Mellor
Caro Millington
Rajiv Nathwani
Stephen Pidcock
James St. Ville KC
Jan Topham
Kit & Anthony van Tulleken
Angela Wachner

CORPORATE SPONSORS
Biznography
Casting Pictures Ltd.
Nick Hern Books
S&P Global
The Agency

TRUSTS & FOUNDATIONS
Backstage Trust
Buffini Chao Foundation
Christina Smith Foundation
Daisy Trust
Esmée Fairbairn Foundation
Garrick Charitable Trust
The Golsoncott Foundation
Hammersmith United Charities
The Headley Trust
Idlewild Trust
Jerwood Foundation
John Lyon's Charity
Martin Bowley Charitable Trust
Noël Coward Foundation
Royal Victoral Hall Foundation
The Thistle Trust

And all the donors who wish to remain anonymous.

If you are interested in finding out how to be involved, please visit **bushtheatre.co.uk/support-us** email **development@bushtheatre.co.uk** or call **020 8743 3584**.

CHARACTERS

JOYCE – ERICA's Mother, ELAINE's Daughter.
ERICA – JOYCE's Daughter, ELAINE's Grandaughter
ELAINE – JOYCE's Mother, ERICA's Grandmother.

TIME

Set in 2025, with flashbacks into our characters' past.

NOTES ON SCRIPT

/ indicates overlapping dialogue

Both actresses play Elaine

AUTHOR'S NOTE

Not Your Superwoman has been a journey that began long before the first draft hit the page. Like many plays, it has lived through workshops, conversations, and rehearsal rooms, reshaping itself each time. It grows out of an experience that I, and many Black women, carry – the expectation to do everything for everyone, often invisibly, while navigating the realities of misogynoir.

This is a play rooted in truth as much as imagination. The birth of my child made me reflect deeply on my family history and my relationship with my parents. It also sent me on a therapy journey, all threads that found their way into Erica's story. As a Black Caribbean woman who grew up in London, I've always been passionate about putting Black British stories on stage, particularly the ones that rarely make it into our theatres. So while this play is fictional, it carries echoes of my lived experience and the many stories I've witnessed and listened to in my community.

For me, theatre is at its most powerful when it creates both recognition and conversation. *Not Your Superwoman* asks us to sit with complexity: the tension between vulnerability and strength, the contradictions of love and frustration, and the humour that coexists with pain. It was essential to me that these women were never reduced to archetypes, but allowed to live fully on stage – flawed, funny, tender, and real.

This play invites you to recognise the weight of expectation that Black women so often carry, and also to celebrate the radical act of laying that weight down.

Above all, *Not Your Superwoman* is a love letter to Black women – our complexity, resilience, and right to exist beyond stereotypes.

ACKNOWLEDGEMENTS

It took a lot of Superwomen to make this play, and I'm so grateful to you all.

Letitia, Golda, and Lynette, thank you for letting this Jamaican gyal be an honorary Guyanese girlie! Together we ploughed through draft after draft, mining these characters and these worlds. I am so incredibly proud of what we've created together.

Dee, your big brain is matched only by your big heart. Your care, consideration, and ability to remind me what this play is truly about pushed me to work at a level I didn't even know I was capable of. I'm a stronger writer because of you.

Amelia, our brilliant Assistant Director – you are truly a marvel. Your integrity, diligence, and depth of research helped shape this show into what it is. Collaborating with you has been a gift, and I can't wait until we get to do it again.

To my wonderful writing agents, Kat Buckle and Jessica Price – working with you is such a joy. Thank you for always believing in me, supporting me, and taking such good care of me.

To the superwomen who have had my back – this play would not exist without you.

Salmah, Shaazia, Karen, Shannon, Tracey, Ash, Chloe, Shereen, Racheal, Somalia, Susan, Faith, Amy, Jennifer, Jordana, Bridget, Dani, Kaila, Tutku, Lara, Cassie, Vicki, Kat W, Elle, Hockley, Cheryl, Lauren, Pernille and Monsay.

Through some of the most challenging times, you have been my Superwomen. This play is as much yours as it is mine – a testament to our resilience, our laughter, and our shared strength. I carry deep gratitude for each of you.

And of course, the Superwoman to whom this play is dedicated: my little sister Maya. You are my Superwoman. I am so incredibly proud of you and the woman you've become. Thank you for simply being you – I honestly don't know what I'd do without you.

For every Superwoman who lifted me up – this play is ours.

To Maya – my Superwoman

One

*(**JOYCE** and **ERICA** are on separate sides of the stage.)*

JOYCE. Flying is one of those things, that's amazing when you're rich. But crap when you're not.

The queueing.

The apps.

I hate the apps.

Why is everything done on a bloody app these days?

If you ask me, it's not been the same since they stopped us from smoking on planes.

Not that I smoke, anymore.

Not touched a fag, this century.

Well, not touched one sober.

I quit smoking.

1999.

The day I got shot of her father.

31st December 1999.

I said to myself – Joyce.

You are walking into the new century fifteen stone lighter.

Fag free and single.

And I did.

Mind you, I did put on two stone once I quit.

ERICA. Ten hours.

That's how long this flight is going to be.

Ten hours.

With my mum.

If I deep it, this will be the most time we've spent together in years.

I was watching a documentary – well a TikTok – and this woman was talking about time blocking.

So like basically, you allocate time to all the different components of your day.

In this case my flight.

So I guess, I speak to my mum, for like ten minutes.

Then we watch the safety presentation – fifteen minutes.

Well more – five minutes.

Then we take off – two minutes.

That takes us up to twenty-two minutes.

Leaving nine hours and / twenty-eight minutes.

JOYCE. / twenty-eight minutes late.

That girl is late for everything.

She was two weeks and one day late for her own birth.

In the end they induced me.

Not pretty

I was in labour for four days.

She really took the piss.

All this Caribbean time nonsense.

She was born in King's College Hospital, Camberwell.

She's not late because she's Black.

She's late because she's fucking inconsiderate.

It's a lack of respect for / people's time.

ERICA. / That's a lot of time.

I could watch a film?

Sinners.

Good film.

But it's a horror.

Vampires.

Blood.

White people.

Terrifying honestly.

Is a horror the right thing to watch when you're like three-thousand feet above the ground?

But Michael B Jordan...times two.

OK, that could run.

JOYCE. This is our first time flying together.

I wasn't allowed to take her on holiday when she was little.

Her father.

Wouldn't give me permission.

I tell this to every woman that will hear me.

Do.

Not.

Put.

That.

Man.

On.

The.

Birth.

Certificate.

It is more trouble than it's worth.

My ex-husband, the first one. I've had two.

Erica's father.

He wasn't interested in travelling.

The only place he wanted to go was Jamaica

His mum lived in one of those ugly huge houses that returnees always buy.

Cast iron gates on the windows,

Scary security dogs.

And ugly DFS furniture.

"Small Island Girl".

That's what she called me.

Guyana is not an island.

You ignorant old bag.

I wanted my daughter to see the world.

But her father made all kinds of threats saying he'd get me done for kidnapping and child abduction.

I couldn't risk it.

Not with my job.

So we just never went anywhere together.

ERICA. I'm going to Guyana!

To spread my Granny's ashes. Lay her to rest.

See what Guyana is about,

Find out more about my family history, family secrets...

(Beat.)

The way I'm going to have to lock in the tools I've learnt in therapy for this holiday.

Whew.

I'm going to make my therapist proud.

She's a Black woman, which is cool because I don't have to explain myself, she just kinda gets it.

But therapy is hard.

Don't get me wrong, I've had some breakthroughs.

But it's a lot.

You know?

JOYCE. Erica's very sensitive, I would say too sensitive / maybe.

ERICA. / With Mum it's like she's missing a sensitivity chip. I don't think she's noticed that I'm not really speaking to her.

JOYCE. She's not really speaking to me.

What you gonna do?

We're both adults!

(An airport.)

*(**ERICA** and **JOYCE** come together face to face with each other.)*

(Beat.)

You reach?

ERICA. Yeah.

>   *(Beat.)*

Sorry, I was late.

There's been a lot going on.

The trains were doing a madness.

JOYCE. Train?

ERICA. Yeah

JOYCE. Didn't Lahnaray drop you?

ERICA. Who?

JOYCE. Your fiancé?

ERICA. Lanre, is working.

>   *(Awkward pause.)*

JOYCE. How's the designing going?

ERICA. Busy, we've got a new contract with the NHS that
we're working on.

JOYCE. So you're working on the website?

ERICA. Mum, I'm not a web designer.

JOYCE. I know that Erica, you do the graphics. You're a
graphics designer.

ERICA. No, I don't. I'm a service and product designer.

JOYCE. Right.

ERICA. I do UX and UI services.

And so the partnership with the NHS is about creating
digital products and services.

JOYCE. Right.

ERICA. Maybe we should go through?

JOYCE. Oh, not that way, I upgraded us.

ERICA. Why did you do that? It's so expensive. I can't pay you back / for that.

JOYCE. / I had points, well not me. Work. The Lawyers. I wouldn't have made you pay.

>*(Beat.)*

Well thanks Mum for sorting.

ERICA. / Thank you

>*(British Airways plane – Business Class.)*

>**(JOYCE** *and* **ERICA** *step on the plane.* **JOYCE** *has two 'welcome drinks',* **ERICA** *has one.)*

JOYCE. ...Emirates you turn left.

Virgin upper class you used to turn left, but on the new planes you go upstairs.

British Airways isn't what it used to be honestly.

ERICA. It's a bit mad that they make you walk past business and premium economy to get to the back of plane.

JOYCE. It's all marketing.

Shaming you into it.

So when you next book, you remember the feeling of walking all the way down to seat 47C.

ERICA. I hear it, I never want to see 47C again in my life.

However HSBC is telling me otherwise.

JOYCE. I can't believe your salary, I don't know how you live on that. Maybe you want to move into what I do? Executive Assistant. Directors and Partners always need someone, I could / always ask.

ERICA. / I'm happy where I'm at.

JOYCE. Are you? For that money?

ERICA. Not everything is about money.

(**ERICA** *spots someone.*)

Oh My God.

JOYCE. What?

ERICA. Don't make it bait.

Central Cee is on the plane.

JOYCE. Who?

ERICA. Central Cee, the rapper.

JOYCE. What that white boy over there?

ERICA. He's not white.

JOYCE. Looks it.

ERICA. He's Guyanese.

JOYCE. Guyanese people can be white you know.

We've got Portuguese in us.

ERICA. I know.

Mum, stop staring.

JOYCE. Are you sure he's a rapper?

ERICA. Yes Mum.

JOYCE. He must be doing alright for himself if he's flying Business.

What's he sing?

ERICA. Loads of songs

JOYCE. Like what?

ERICA. Probably nothing you would have heard.

JOYCE. How do you know?

I know music, you know!

What's his big hit?

ERICA. He's got a song with Dave.

JOYCE. Dave? Who you went sixth form with?

ERICA. Not Dave I went sixth form with Dave the rapper.

JOYCE. Didn't Dave who you went sixth form with rap?

ERICA. I mean, a bit but – Never mind.

JOYCE. Well how does the song go, the one with Dave?

> (**ERICA** *quietly sings along the chorus of "Sprinter" by Central Cee and Dave.*[*])

Never heard of it.

ERICA. Told you didn't I?

JOYCE. You're probably singing it wrong.

> (**JOYCE** *is tapping on her phone.*)

Oh it's C with two Ees.

Ceeeee.

> (*"Band4Band" by Central Cee plays on* **JOYCE**'s *phone – loudly.*[*])

ERICA. What are you / doing?

JOYCE. Oh, didn't mean / to do that.

ERICA. This is so / embarrassing.

JOYCE. How do I / turn this off.

---

[*] A licence to produce *Not Your Superwoman* does not include a performance licence for any third-party or copyrighted music or copyrighted recordings. Licensees should create an original composition or use music in the public domain. For further information, please see the Music and Third-Party Materials Use Note on page iii

ERICA. Mum, turn / that off.

JOYCE. I'm trying.

>   (**ERICA** *grabs* **JOYCE***'s phone and turns it off.*)

ERICA. Oh my God.

JOYCE. I hate to be one of those people but I'm just going to say it, they don't make music like they used to.

>   *(Beat.)*

Oh *Sinners*.

Michael B Jordan...times two.

Should we watch it together?

Like we'll press play at the same time.

ERICA. Sure, why not.

JOYCE. Are you going to drink your welcome drink?

ERICA. I'm actually reassessing my relationship with alcohol.

JOYCE. Oh right. Good for you. Can I have it?

>   (**ERICA** *hands over her drink.)*

Cheers.

ERICA. To Granny.

JOYCE. Well she's the reason why we're here.

Didn't see myself going to Guyana anytime soon.

ERICA. Really?

JOYCE. I've not got any relatives there and there's no beaches, so what am I there for?

>   *(The flight departs.)*

(**ERICA** and **JOYCE** *go through the transitions of a long flight, toilet breaks, eating, watching films, falling asleep.)*

Two

(Hotel Room.)

(Enter **JOYCE** *and* **ERICA**.*)*

*(***ERICA*** *opens her hand luggage and takes out three zip lock bags full of ashes.)*

JOYCE. Not much of a suite is it? We're here!

ERICA. *(Speaking to the zip lock bags.)* We're here. Granny, we made it.

JOYCE. You put my mum in zip lock bags?

ERICA. I needed something discreet

JOYCE. Discreet? Looks like packets of bloody hash or something.

You're lucky we never got stopped.

ERICA. Well it's done now. All good.

*(***ERICA*** *holds the zip lock bags.)*

Granny, we are going to take you to all the places we talked about.

*(***ERICA*** *kisses the zip lock bags.)*

JOYCE. Babe, you know she's not really there.

Like you're kissing a zip lock bag of remains.

ERICA. It's all I've got left of her.

*(***ERICA*** *is emotional and* ***JOYCE***, *unsure of what to do, settles for a pat on* ***ERICA***'s *shoulder.)*

Sorry, there's been a lot of travelling.

JOYCE. Yeah, exactly. You probably just need to rest.

(Beat.)

Not much of a suite is it?

ERICA. I've never stayed in a suite before, so I wouldn't know.

JOYCE. Didn't Lahnaray /

ERICA. / It's Lanre. Lan-REE

JOYCE. Sorry. Lan-REE. Don't the two of you holiday together?

ERICA. Yeah, but we mainly did Airbnbs, not hotels – so no suites.

(Waves away a mosquito.)

JOYCE. Jeez, these mosquitos...

ERICA. EATING ME ALIVE, man.

(Beat.)

Shall we run through the itinerary?

JOYCE. Sure.

ERICA. Granny asked for her ashes to be spread in three spots.

Kaieteur Falls because it's the most beautiful place in Guyana and her Grandmother's grave so they can be back together.

JOYCE. Great.

ERICA. And for the last one – Thursday is the one year anniversary of her death and I think it would be cool if we spread the rest of her ashes at / Ranjani's.

JOYCE. / The general store?

ERICA. Yeah.

JOYCE. / I get the other two, but why would you spread her ashes there?

ERICA. It's part of our family legacy, we owned that store for generations. It's a family landmark. Do you have another suggestion?

JOYCE. No.

ERICA. It's gotta be places she connected with, Mum.

This is important.

So three p.m. Thursday.

We should also visit the Seawall.

And there's a creek that looks really cool.

It's about a forty-five minute drive from here.

I also thought that we could look at the Museum of African Heritage / which isn't too far from...

JOYCE. / Any chance we could do something fun?

ERICA. I've scheduled in lots of free time.

JOYCE. Good to hear it.

> (*JOYCE begins unpacking.*)

Lanre!

ERICA. Sorry what?

JOYCE. That's how you pronounce it right?

ERICA. Yes Mum, that's how you pronounce it.

> (*JOYCE continues unpacking.*)

JOYCE. Have you contacted him to let him know you've arrived?

ERICA. No

> (*Beat.*)

We're not together.

(**JOYCE** *stops unpacking turns to* **ERICA**.)

JOYCE. Whatever you do, don't give back that ring. Remember that VW Golf I used to drive? Brought that when I sold the engagement ring your father got me. Better investment in the long run.

(*Beat.*)

They're all fuckers. The lot of them. That Lah-nah, Lan, whatever his fucking name is, is a grubworm.

(*Beat.*)

ERICA. Grubworm?

JOYCE. Oh I don't know. Couldn't think of another word.

(**ERICA** *laughs.*)

He cheated didn't he?

ERICA. Not that I know of.

JOYCE. So why did you break up?

ERICA. I think in the end we just weren't compatible.

(*Beat.*)

There was a distance between us.

JOYCE. What does that mean?

ERICA. It just didn't work out.

JOYCE. Do you know what I reckon? It's the curse.

ERICA. Here we go again…

JOYCE. You know I'm not into all that witchy witchy foolishness, but you know how the story goes.

ERICA. One of the ancestors back in the day was a bit of a sexy lady.

JOYCE. And she got jiggy with someone's husband /and

ERICA. /And then his wife of the husband went to an Obeah woman.

ERICA & JOYCE. Cursed our whole bloodline.

JOYCE. It's the only explanation!

ERICA. That's the only explanation?

Not unhealed trauma?

Unhealthy relationship patterns?

Just Obeah?

> *(Beat.)*

JOYCE. I'm thirsty, are you?

ERICA. I think there might be some complimentary water in that mini fridge.

JOYCE. I don't want that, I want a proper drink. Let's pop out.

ERICA. Alright, I'll just have the one.

JOYCE. Yeah man. Let's hang out catch a vibe.

ERICA. Shall I google some local spots?

JOYCE. We are two single British women in Guyana, we can't just wander around.

There's a hotel bar. We'll start there.

Three

(Hotel Bar.)

("Lucy" by Destra Garcia plays.*)

*(**JOYCE** and **ERICA** are catching a vibe.)*

JOYCE. This El Dorado and apple juice got me feeling nice.

You want another?

ERICA. I've had my one. Music is lit though. Soca to the world!!

JOYCE. I'm going to start ordering two at a time.

Gandhi is so slow.

ERICA. Who's Gandhi?

JOYCE. The barman.

ERICA. How do you know his name?

JOYCE. You always want to know the name of the hotel barman.

It's how you get premium luxury service.

ERICA. You get premium luxury service because you pay for it.

JOYCE. Partly, but it's also how they interact with people. I'll give you an example.

So you go to a nice bar or restaurant right?

And you say to the waiter, what's your name?

(Beat.)

---

* A licence to produce *Not Your Superwoman* does not include a performance licence for any third-party or copyrighted recordings. Licensees should create their own.

JOYCE. Well go on answer?

ERICA. My name? Erm... Erica.

JOYCE. Make up a name, we're roleplaying.

ERICA. OK... Sabrina?

JOYCE. Gorgeous, "Sabrina, so lovely to meet you. I'm Joyce."

So, throughout the meal I make sure I interact you.

"Thank you Sabrina."

"Sabrina, sorry to bother you, where's the bathroom?"

"What do you recommend Sabrina?"

That kind of thing.

End of the night.

I give you a tip and say,

"It's been so lovely meeting you Sabrina, I really hope to see you soon".

And you say,

"Lovely to meet you too Joyce thanks for the tip."

Now the tip is honestly quite modest, but it's the way you've made her feel.

Sabrina feels seen.

Sabrina feels heard.

ERICA. Sabrina feel understood.

Mum, I –

JOYCE. Right. Shots!

El Dorado neat, please Gandhi.

ERICA. You are insane

JOYCE. And you love it.

(Two shots of Eldorado appear.)

To Mummy.

*(**JOYCE** drinks her shot.)*

ERICA. To Granny.

*(**ERICA** pours her shot on the floor.)*

JOYCE. What'd you do that for?

ERICA. It's a libation, for Granny.

JOYCE. She didn't even drink, apart from her annual Christmas Eve sherry. Now poor old Gandhi's got to clean / that up.

ERICA. I just thought /

JOYCE. / waste of good Rum.

What are you like?

("Carnival" by Destra Garcia and Machel Montano plays. **ERICA** and **JOYCE** react to the song. Joyous.)*

Nah.

This is my choon.

Gandhi turn this one up!

(The music get louder.)

ERICA. Bad man tune!

(The music gets even louder.)

Wooooiiiiiiii

(Sings along.)

---

* A licence to produce *Not Your Superwoman* does not include a performance licence for any third-party or copyrighted recordings. Licensees should create their own.

ERICA. I love this song.

ERICA. Same!

JOYCE. Notting Hill Carnival remember babe?
2005?

ERICA. No, 2003.

JOYCE. That long ago?

ERICA. You had them adidas shorts on.

JOYCE. PumPum shorts yeah?

ERICA. Yeah

JOYCE. Sounds about right.

ERICA. And I had matching ones, not shorts, jogging
bottoms.

What a song man!

> (**JOYCE** *dances and* **ERICA** *joins her.*)

> (*Feet dancing, bums shaking, pure
> unabandoned unfiltered joy.*)

> (*The music fades.*)

> (*Time passes.*)

> (*The lights turn down.*)

> (*The end of the night songs start to play.*)

> (*"How Do I Live" by LeAnn Rimes.**)

> (**JOYCE** *drunkenly sings a few lines.* **ERICA**
> *joins in.*)

---

* A licence to produce *Not Your Superwoman* does not include a
performance licence for any third-party or copyrighted recordings.
Licensees should create their own.

JOYCE. I'm telling you, you love to stop my fun.

Being a mum is a thankless task.

Ever since you were an embryo making me throw up all day.

(Hotel Room.)

*(Enter **ERICA** and **JOYCE**.)*

*(**JOYCE** starts rolling up a spliff.)*

ERICA. What are you doing?

JOYCE. What does it look like I'm doing?

ERICA. Where did you even get that?

JOYCE. Gandhi.

*(**JOYCE** lights up and takes a puff.)*

ERICA. I really would rather that you didn't smoke in the room.

JOYCE. Do us a favour babe, come here. Turn around.

*(**ERICA** turns around and **JOYCE** mimes taking a stick out of her bottom.)*

ERICA. What are you doing?

JOYCE. Taking that giant stick out your arse.

ERICA. Mum, you're too old for / this.

JOYCE. Less of the old please and thank you.

ERICA. You're drunk.

JOYCE. I'm on holiday, I meant to be drunk!

Why aren't you drunk?

Because you're 'reevaluating your relationship with alcohol'.

ERICA. Reassessing.

>(**ERICA** *turns on the TV.* **JOYCE** *takes a puff.*)

>(*A rerun of the sitcom "One on One" plays.**)

JOYCE. Turn it off.

>(**ERICA** *continues watching ignoring* **JOYCE**.)

Turn it off.

>(**ERICA** *continues to ignore* **JOYCE**.)

I said. Turn it off.

>(**JOYCE** *pulls the plug out of the wall.*)

ERICA. What are you doing?

>(**JOYCE** *exits to the bathroom almost in a trance like state.*)

Mum? Mum?

>(***Flashback [2006].***)

>(**JOYCE**'s *flat.*)

>(*Bathroom.*)

>(**JOYCE** *[36] and* **ELAINE** *[55] face each other.*)

JOYCE. There was no heartbeat at the scan.

They reckon it stopped growing around five weeks.

They said they could remove it surgically in a week or that maybe I can DIY it.

---

* A licence to produce *Not Your Superwoman* does not include a performance licence for any third-party or copyrighted recordings or images. Licensees must acquire rights for any copyrighted recordings or images or create their own.

So they suggested that I take these tablets to...make it happen.

(**ELAINE** *hands* **JOYCE** *a glass of water.*)

ELAINE. Take the pills Joyce, I'm here now.

(**ELAINE** *takes out some pills swallows them and then drinks the glass of water.*)

What he saying?

JOYCE. He's gone to Liverpool

To his mum's.

ELAINE. Men, they never know what fi do in these circumstances

JOYCE. Well something would have been better than nothing.

I thought Sean was different to Erica's father.

How could I get it so wrong, twice?

ELAINE. Is di woman, di woman from Parika. She work Obeah pon the women in the family.

JOYCE. Not that again.

ELAINE. I tell you dis story already?

JOYCE. Yes mummy, all the women in our family are cursed.

(*They fall silent as they hear "One on One" theme tune playing on the television.**)

ELAINE. She know?

JOYCE. No.

---

* A licence to produce *Not Your Superwoman* does not include a performance licence for any third-party or copyrighted recordings or images. Licensees must acquire rights for any copyrighted recordings or images or create their own.

ELAINE. Keep it like that. She's still a little baby.

JOYCE. She's eleven. Not a baby

ELAINE. You've got to protect she.

This is big people business, you know. No place for a child.

Is you burden. You carry it alone.

>   (**JOYCE** *clutches her stomach in pain.*)

>   (*Beat.*)

JOYCE. It hurts. Mummy it hurts.

ELAINE. God would never put anything on your plate that you can't manage.

So it go.

>   (*Exit* **ELAINE**.)

>   (**JOYCE** *sits on the toilet, as her pregnancy passes.*)

>   (**JOYCE** *wipes, there's blood.*)

>   (*The sound of the "One on One" theme tune plays louder and louder invasive in her mind.**)

>   (*The flashback fades and we are back in the present day.*)

ERICA. Mum

>   (*Beat.*)

Mum, I need to know you're alive in there.

---

* A licence to produce *Not Your Superwoman* does not include a performance licence for any third-party or copyrighted recordings or images. Licensees must acquire rights for any copyrighted recordings or images or create their own.

(Beat.)

Can you confirm that you're alive?

(Beat.)

Fine, I'm calling Gandhi to break down the door.

JOYCE. Oh, for God's sake.

ERICA. I heard that. So I take it, you're OK?

JOYCE. I'm fine.

(Beat.)

I'm going to sleep in here.

ERICA. Don't be stupid.

JOYCE. In the bath.

ERICA. No, you're not.

JOYCE. Night.

> (**JOYCE** *climbs into the bath and goes to sleep.)*

ERICA. Wait Mum, are you being serious?

JOYCE. So it go.

Enjoy the bed.

> (**JOYCE** *falls asleep in the bath.)*
>
> (**JOYCE***'s dream – flashes of a fragment of a Guyanese Childhood.)*
>
> *(The colours are saturated and blurry.)*
>
> *(Sounds of boots on a wooden floor. Male voices.)*
>
> (**JOYCE** *wakes up in the bath, unsettled.)*

Four

(Airport runway.)

*(**JOYCE** and **ERICA** are about to board a small aircraft.)*

JOYCE. I am hanging.

I didn't think this one through.

Why you signed us up for this, I will never understand. Utter foolishness.

ERICA. You know why we're doing this and what it's for. It's for her.

JOYCE. That woman.

(Beat.)

Fine, quickly before I change my mind.

*(**ERICA** and **JOYCE** step onto the plane.)*

(The plane moves off.)

Our father, who art in heaven

Hallowed be thy name, thy kingdom come.

ERICA. Mum, please.

JOYCE. Thy will be done.

ERICA. Seriously?

JOYCE. Give us this day our daily bread.

And forgive us our trespasses.

ERICA. Mum you've got to see this. Look out the window.

JOYCE. As we forgive those who trespass / against us.

ERICA. Mum it's incredible.

*(**JOYCE** and **ERICA** look at the window and get a first glimpse of Kaieteur Falls.)*

JOYCE. Rarse!

ERICA. I can't believe it.

It's…it's like we're at the edge of the earth.

JOYCE. Kaieteur fucking Falls.

ERICA. You realise how small you are.

JOYCE. I'm no stranger to travel, but this feels like another level.

I've seen the pyramids.

Taj Mahal.

And the Colosseum.

I'm stunned.

ERICA. This is why Granny wanted us to come home.

JOYCE. Maybe…

*(The plane lands and **ERICA** and **JOYCE** get off.)*

*(**ERICA** carefully takes out one of the zip lock bags.)*

ERICA. I think we should do it, like over the ridge.

JOYCE. Oh, so you want us all to die?

*(**ERICA** offers her hand to **JOYCE** who takes it and grips hard, carefully they walk to the ridge.)*

ERICA. Granny, we made it. Your prayers have been answered and you are finally here. It's more beautiful than I could have ever imagined. I'm so glad that a piece of you will always be here

JOYCE. Nice.

ERICA. I actually wrote a few words.

>*(Beat.)*

As these ashes scatter into the wind,

so too does your essence return to the world –

to the waterfall, to the sky, to the trees.

You are everywhere now, and always with us.

>*(Beat.)*

Did you want to say a few words Mum?

JOYCE. Not after that.

>*(**ERICA** puts her hand in the zip lock bag and takes out a fistful of ashes, which she throws out, the wind blows them back on her.)*

Oh shit.

>*(Beat. Then laughter from **JOYCE**.)*

It's not funny.

I think I swallowed some.

>*(This makes **JOYCE** laugh even more. **ERICA** laughs too. As the laughter subsides they both look out towards the waterfall – a silence falls between them. **JOYCE** takes the zip lock bag from **ERICA** and grabs a handful of ashes, and instead of throwing it lets them pour out of her fist, over the ridge. **ERICA** takes a fistful of ashes and does the same.)*

>*(**Flashback [2006]**.)*

>*(Elaine's house.)*

(**ELAINE** *[55] is doing some alterations to some carnival outfits using* **ERICA** *[11] as a fit model.*)

ERICA. Why does Mum always go on holiday, when I'm at school? Other people's mum wait until the holidays, so that they can go together.

ELAINE. Erica, it's very complicated. One day when you're older you'll understand.

ERICA. You always say that.

ELAINE. Because it's true.

(*Beat.*)

What about if me and you went on a holiday? Just us.

ERICA. To where?

ELAINE. Where else?

ERICA. Guyana?

ERICA. Will we visit your grandma's shop?

ELAINE. What Ranjani's?

I don't even know if it's still there.

I ever tell you that my Grandad came up with the name Ranjani?

He make up an Indian sounding name so that Indian people would think it was an Indian store and come in. And it worked. Every type of person went there. Black, Portugese, Indian.

The most successful general store in the whole district.

And we built it.

Our family built it.

On our land...

ELAINE. But you know where we have to go…Kaieteur Falls. You can't go all the way to Guyana without going to Kaieteur Falls.

ERICA. What's that?

ELAINE. A big big waterfall.

You've got to get a seaplane there.

ERICA. Won't you be scared? You don't like flying.

ELAINE. But I'll have you and when I've got you, I can do anything.

> *(The sound of the waterfall as the flashback fades away and we are left with* **ERICA** *and* **JOYCE** *staring out at Kaieteur Falls.)*

ERICA. I can't believe she never got a chance to see this. She would have loved it.

> *(***ERICA*** takes out a bottle of rum.)*

JOYCE. What happened to reassessing your relationship with alcohol?

ERICA. It's not for me, it's for Granny.

To the best Granny in the world.

We love you.

> *(***ERICA*** pours out a libation for Granny.)*

Mum, I've got to tell you something.

JOYCE. I'm all ears.

> *(Beat.)*

ERICA. I'm glad we did this. Together.

JOYCE. Yeah me too.

ERICA. I'm going to check on our ride back.

JOYCE. OK.

> (**ERICA** *heads down to return to the plane and*
> **JOYCE** *stays for a moment.*)

It's actually going quite well.

Don't want to jinx it but yeah.

I'm fucking buzzing.

It was the right thing to do, coming here. I have done the right thing. For once.

This place makes me feel level.

And I need that.

Haven't been feeling myself for a while

Even before Mummy died and eighteen months ago there was a point I was just not quite –

I don't know.

I'd been on a business trip and when I came back I just sort of sat down and lost myself.

I missed everything that week, my book club, my spa date, even Erica's engagement party.

I wanted to be there.

Of course I did.

I ordered a nice little coral French Connection number.

And then...

I just couldn't.

We haven't really been the same since then.

So it go.

> (*Sounds of men, footsteps, voices.*)

Keep it together Joyce – keep a lid on it, get through the trip and then take some time off. That's all you need.

Rest.

Don't spiral. Not in front of her. Keep your shit together.

Five

(The next day. **ERICA** *and* **JOYCE** *have ventured to a local food shop.*

*(***ERICA*** *is confident in her surroundings,* **JOYCE** *is not.)*

ERICA. Could I get some bake and salt fish please? Maybe some roti? What you having?

JOYCE. Um…

(She spots the cheese rolls.)

One of them. Can I have a cheese roll?

*(***JOYCE*** *takes a cheese roll and bites into it. It's good melt in your mouth, good.)*

Diabetes and high blood pressure in a flaky cheesy pastry.

Yum.

Me and Mummy used to make these.

ERICA. You cooked?

JOYCE. Yes.

Why you look so surprised?

Every Sunday.

*(**Flashback [1980].**)*

*(***JOYCE*** *[10] is eating a cheese roll.)*

JOYCE. Mummy, where is my daddy?

ELAINE. Don't talk with your mouth full.

(*JOYCE quickly chews and then swallows and doesn't miss a beat continuing like she never stopped talking.*)

JOYCE. The kids at school ask me, why I don't have a daddy and if he have funny voice like you.

ELAINE. Nothing is wrong with my voice. But you just make sure that you talk good and clear.

JOYCE. What about my daddy?

Where is he?

ELAINE. He's away.

JOYCE. In Guyana?

ELAINE. America.

JOYCE. Why is he in America?

ELAINE. He has an important job to do there.

JOYCE. Like a superhero?

ELAINE. Something like that.

JOYCE. My daddy is a superhero? So he can come here and save me when the other kids tease me?

ELAINE. No one is coming to save you baby girl, you have to save yourself.

JOYCE. Like Supergirl? And when I grow up, I'll be superwoman!

I think we're superheroes and no one is supposed to know.

Are we Mummy?

ELAINE. Joyce – yuh ask too much question. Go look your book.

(*Fade to present day,* **JOYCE** *is watching* **ERICA** *ordering more food.*)

ERICA. And a cane juice? Mm Pholourie, let's get some of that too!

JOYCE. Slow down Erica...

ERICA. Don't food shame me!

And I'll also have a cheese roll –

JOYCE. We missed a trick not having these at the funeral –

ERICA. 'WE' missed a trick?

JOYCE. Mummy loved them. We never served any at the wake.

ERICA. Well maybe if you had helped organise it –

JOYCE. I paid for it –

ERICA. Yes we know, you pay for everything –

JOYCE. There would have been no real funeral if it wasn't for me, the money I spent –

ERICA. Really mum? We gonna do this here?

> *(Beat.)*

I don't want to argue – let's just have a nice day.

> *(**ERICA** bites into the cheese roll.)*

> *(**Flashback [1999].**)*

> *(**ERICA** [4] is eating a cheese roll talking to **ELAINE**.)*

ERICA. Granny, why is mum always in bed?

ELAINE. What you talking about child?

ERICA. She says she feels sick, but I just think she's being boring.

ELAINE. Don't be rude about your mother.

ERICA. But Granny it's true, she's always in bed.

Sometimes she's in bed all day, and I get hungry and my tummy rumbles.

So maybe she doesn't love me anymore

Just like Dad.

ELAINE. Your mother loves you.

Don't worry about your father. It's big people business Erica, you'll understand one day when you're older.

ERICA. Granny, how comes I always sleep at your house, instead of at home with Mummy?

ELAINE. Erica – Yuh ask too much question. Go look your book.

ERICA. Fine, but I'm taking a cheese roll.

I feel sick Granny –

> *(Back to the present day.)*

> (**ERICA** *suddenly and violently throws up.*)

JOYCE. Oh God, No. Don't do that.

> (**ERICA** *throws up some more.* **JOYCE** *is queasy.)*

I'm just going to stand here, while you – yeah.

ERICA. Maybe I overdid it with all that food.

JOYCE. Told you to slow down.

Oh.

ERICA. Mum?

JOYCE. Last night I dreamt fish.

Six

(Hotel bathroom.)

*(**ERICA** awaits the results of her pregnancy test.)*

ERICA. I check my phone.

Health app.

Last period...

Last one...

Fifty-four days ago.

I've never been regular, but fifty-four days is diabolical.

I've been stressed.

I've been doing a lot.

My body is under pressure So it could be nothing.

So here I am.

Peeing on a stick.

OK one line. Cute.

That's what I'm talking about!

*(Enter **JOYCE**.)*

JOYCE. You good?

ERICA. I'm fucking amazing

*(**JOYCE** and **ERICA** do a celebration dance.)*

JOYCE. Oh my God, negative. Thank fuck for that.

Otherwise you'd be stuck with that bloody man for the rest of your life.

*(**ERICA** picks up the test to throw it away –*
freezes when she notices something.)

ERICA. Wait a minute.

This is not happening.

*(**JOYCE** grabs the test.)*

JOYCE. I mean it's very faint.

ERICA. So you see it too?

JOYCE. Let me put my glasses on.

(Gets glasses out.)

Yeh.

(Beat.)

I'm sorry babe.

ERICA. I don't know what to do.

JOYCE. You do, but you just got to block out the outside
noise.

(Beat.)

ERICA. Fucking pregnant! How and when did that happen?

JOYCE. I think you're a little too old for the birds and the
bees conversation...

ERICA. I can't deal with this right now, I just want to get on
with what we came here to do. Next stop, the museum
of African Heritage...

JOYCE. Whatever you want Babe. I'll go call the driver.

*(Exit **JOYCE**.)*

*(A moment as **ERICA** gathers her thoughts.)*

ERICA. This is not it.

This is...

Stupid.

Lanre's barely fucking touched me.

We've had no accidents or slip ups apart from...

(Beat.)

oh yea, there was that one time...

(Beat.)

That was a good time!

A really good time.

But this is not part of the plan.

We're not even together.

I don't know what to do that.

(Beat.)

Fucking get your shit together Erica.

This is not the time to start spiralling.

Especially not in front of her.

This is about Granny and doing what needs to be done.

Hold it in.

I've gotta hold this shit together.

Seven

(Le Repentir Cemetery. A day later.)

*(**JOYCE** and **ERICA** are searching for a grave. **ERICA** is distracted, still reeling on her pregnancy news. **JOYCE** is at her wit's end.)*

JOYCE. Erica, slow down, isn't there a map or something?

ERICA. Nah, Granny just left very vague directions.

JOYCE. *(Does an impression of **ELAINE**.)* Up suh, round suh, near one Bush.

ERICA. Bingo.

JOYCE. You found it?

ERICA. I've found the Grants.

JOYCE. There's so many Grants.

ERICA. Sunrise 1925. Sunset 2024. Ah man, so close to the big one hundred.

JOYCE. Can you imagine making it that close to one hundred – and then dying?

ERICA. I'd be so vex.

JOYCE. I'd be in that grave, FUMING!

ERICA. You know what I'm clocking, all the women in our family don't make it much past their sixties. I thought Granny was young at seventy-three but compared to the women in her family – she lived a good age.

JOYCE. Probably because she didn't have a husband to stress her out. Married men live longer than single men and single women live longer then married women. It's a fact, I read it in the *Metro*.

*(**ERICA** stops at a grave.)*

ERICA. Darlene Grant. I never heard Granny mention anyone called Darlene. I wonder who she was....maybe our great great great aunt or something? Mad!

(**JOYCE** *is looking at another grave.*)

JOYCE. These ones always make me feel sad.

Why does a four-year-old need to die?

ERICA. Granny would say it was God taking home his angels. Sounded nice when I was little, but I don't know if I believe that anymore.

JOYCE. Me either.

ERICA. I can feel something though.

Being here.

Like surrounded by all of our ancestors you know.

All the Grants that came before us.

Can you feel it too?

(*Beat.*)

JOYCE. Not really, babe.

I think I found her Grandmother though...Norma E Grant. Born 17th December 1912.

Died 9th February 1969.

ERICA. That's her.

My great, great grandmother.

I used to love looking at that picture of her on her bedside dresser. The two of them outside Ranjani's.

Granny looked just like her.

JOYCE. Same eyebrows and nose

ERICA. Granny said she was strict though, and didn't mess around.

JOYCE. She definitely had that look about her.

   (Beat.)

I wish I'd met her, she died when Mummy was pregnant with me. Cancer got her in the end, Mummy said.

ERICA. "as one gaan, the next one born."

   (Beat.)

Kartel innit.

JOYCE. Really? You want to do Vybz Kartel lyrics before we bury my mum's ashes.

You run out of self-penned speeches?

ERICA. Don't worry about me, I got something.

   (Beat.)

When Granny lost her parents, you took her in whilst keeping the family business thriving. You laid her foundations and it's my greatest honour to reunite you both.

   *(**ERICA** takes a small rum out of her bag and pours a libation. **JOYCE** rolls her eyes.)*

Granny was named after her you know. The E stands for Elaine.

JOYCE. I didn't know that.

ERICA. Yup. Apparently she was tall and strong like an ox. Like proper strong. She pushed out her oldest daughter, Granny's Mum, with one push, ate her lunch and went down to Ranjani's to open the store. What a G

JOYCE. How do you know all that?

ERICA. Granny told me so many stories…at the end. Before her memory started to go. She had to get it all out.

JOYCE. Oh really?

ERICA. It was like she was re living everything. It was nice to see her open up more about herself. Yeah she would talk for hours.

(*Flashback [2023].*)

(**ERICA** *is oiling and braiding* **ELAINE**'s *hair.*)

ELAINE. Let me tell you about Guyana.

And the Seawall .

And Fitzroy

ERICA. Who?

ELAINE. Fitzroy. But everyone call him Bruce.

ERICA. Is that Mum's Dad? Fitzroy! What's his surname.

ELAINE. Why you want to know his surname?

This is big people business. Leave it alone, Joyce.

ERICA. It's Erica, Granny.

ELAINE. Joyce?

ERICA. No, Erica. Erica your granddaughter. Joyce's daughter.

ELAINE. Mi glad to see you. You just reach?

(*Beat.*)

ERICA. No, I've been here a little while. I'm doing your hair remember?

(**ERICA** *continues doing* **ELAINE**'s *hair.*)

You should have a pickney.

ERICA. Should I?

ELAINE. Yes a lickle baby girl, name after me.

(*Beat.*)

ELAINE. I don't want to leave this earth without seeing you be a mother.

ERICA. Well one step at a time. Remember, you've got to walk me down that aisle first.

> *(Beat.)*

ELAINE. He used to come to Ranjani's.

ERICA. Who?

ELAINE. Yes,I liked his jet black hair with a wave and his skin.

Oh his skin.

Smooth and brown.

I liked that he was so polite.

Him serious though.

So handsome he would make you forget.

Forget yuh name. Forget yuh job. Forget he had a wife...

ERICA. Granny I –

ELAINE. Gomes. That was his surname. Fitzroy Gomes.

Joycey that's your father's name.

I sorry, I never tell yuh dat before.

> *(The flashback fades and returns to the present day.)*

ERICA. Your dad's in Guyana.

JOYCE. I don't have a dad babe.

ERICA. His name is Fitzroy Gomes, and he lives just outside Georgetown.

JOYCE. No he went to America, whilst she was pregnant and never came back.

ERICA. No.

Granny just told you that.

Truth is your dad has a family.

JOYCE. What are you talking about?

ERICA. And I think that Granny knew that

And that he wasn't going to leave his wife.

(*Beat.*)

I know this is a lot to / digest.

JOYCE. So you're saying she lied to me? All these years.

ERICA. I think she was trying to protect you.

JOYCE. From what? The truth?

ERICA. You were so young, it would have been complicated.

JOYCE. God, you sound just like her.

ERICA. Granny would never do anything to hurt you on purpose.

JOYCE. You have no idea who she really was.

ERICA. I did know who she was. And so did you.

Look, we're in Guyana...

We're home mum, and your dad is –

He's – he's still alive... it's amazing...

JOYCE. Amazing for who? You or me?

ERICA. You get to meet your dad. And I get to meet my grandad. Especially now we've lost granny, /I think –

JOYCE. /No. That man is not my father. I don't care who he is.

ERICA. Of course you care –

JOYCE. Don't tell me how I'm supposed to feel Erica, I have zero interest in a man who has zero interest in me.

ERICA. I just / thought-

JOYCE. / What? What did you think?

ERICA. Maybe you wanted to know more about half yourself?

JOYCE. I'm not half anything.

I'm a whole Joyce.

ERICA. It might be healing for you...

JOYCE. Don't start that shit /

ERICA. / Because for me, when I found him –

JOYCE. / No, what did you just say? You found him?

What do you mean *You* found him?

(*Beat.*)

ERICA. Granny only gave me his name. I researched the rest.

JOYCE. Oh, well, claps for Nancy fucking Drew!

(*Beat.*)

How long have you known about this man?

ERICA. Why does it matter? Can we just focus / on –

JOYCE. HOW LONG ERICA?

ERICA. Like a year ago.

JOYCE. Why would you keep that from / me.

ERICA. / Because we were coming here and Angela, my therapist said it would be good for us to –

JOYCE. Your therapist? You're chatting my business to a stranger?

ERICA. It's not just your business! I'm trying to sort out the shit that I went through as a kid, but I end up working through your shit as well.

JOYCE. What shit did you go through? You got a great education – I paid for everything –

ERICA. Why do you have to remind me of that all the time? You paid for everything. You're my mum!

> *(**Flashback** [1982].)*
>
> *(Elaine's house.)*
>
> *(**JOYCE** [12] is sobbing. **ELAINE** is standing, watching, her arms folded, defensive.)*

JOYCE. Where's my money?

ELAINE. I had to put it on the electricity key. Not now...

JOYCE. But it was mine that I earned doing my paper round.

ELAINE. You want the house to black out again?

I had to pay the bills Erica!

Is just me taking care of everything.

JOYCE. I was saving it Mummy.

I thought I could take us to Guyana/.

ELAINE. / Paper round money not going to carry us back to Guyana.

Why you want to go back there anyways?

JOYCE. I just thought if you were home, you wouldn't be so sad all the time.

ELAINE. Who told you I'm sad?

I'm tired.

I is working all the hours God send.

ELAINE. To keep a roof over we heads.

Be grateful, Joyce!

(Flashback fades into present day.)

JOYCE. You should be fucking grateful, Erica!

ERICA. Don't talk to me like that.

You're mad disrespectful.

JOYCE. Disrespectful? I'm your mother!

ERICA. Rah! Only when you wanna be – you pick, and choose when you want to be a Mum.

JOYCE. I've been your mother for thirty years, whether I've liked it or not – If I could fucking choose, you think I would choose this?

ERICA. Of course you wouldn't. Because it's all about you isn't it? You're a narcissist!

JOYCE. A narcissist? That is fucking rich coming from you when you haven't had to sacrifice a thing in your life.

*(**Flashback [1988].**)*

(Elaine's house.)

ELAINE. What kind of job you going to do with an English Literature degree?

JOYCE. I – I don't know yet. I guess I'll figure it out while I'm studying. There are so many careers you can get with a degree.

I really want this Mum, and I think I've got a shot.

(Beat.)

ELAINE. You've got a good job lined up after college. Law firm. Nice office. Good money. You can / save.

JOYCE. I don't want to do that – this is my passion.

ELAINE. You can't chase passion – you need a good secure foundation to build on.

I didn't fly across the Atlantic for you to read books for three years.

JOYCE. Please / Mummy.

ELAINE. / No. I'm not supporting any more studying.

End of story.

You need to start pulling your weight. It's time to grow up, Joyce.

(Flashback fades back into present day.)

JOYCE. You need to grow up Erica. All the opportunities you've had. Take some responsibility for your own life.

ERICA. Oh cool. I take responsibility. I'll take responsibility for both of us. I pick up all your slack, sort everything out, and better yet I'll just dash money it, because that's what you do –

And this is exactly why Granny didn't tell you shit – everything is a fight, everyone's against you, innit. Do you know what – I'm glad you didn't show your face at the end, poisoning her last days on earth.

JOYCE. Oh there she is.

All this therapy can't cover up who you really are – Look at you –

ERICA. Yeah, yeah Look at me... This is what you made, And guess what mum? I'm going to keep working on myself, chatting your business, and if you want to pay for something, pay for that.

I'm out. Find your own way around Georgetown.

Eight

(**JOYCE** *is wandering around the street in a rage.*)

JOYCE. All I have done Erica's whole life is support. Supported, all her decisions. And for what?

To spend a year fucking plotting and planning.

Behind my back

(*Beat.*)

I haven't needed him for fifty-five fucking years, why would I need him now I'm a grown ass woman.

I always knew Mummy knew more about my father than she told me. I always knew that she had lied. Deep down. Of course she did.

Not even a fucking piece of me that wants to meet that man. I've never needed a dad.

Mummy raised me. Alone.

I just – I just can't believe Erica would do that –

A year, a fucking year. Planning and plotting.

Behind my back.

Fucking 'healing journey'... do you think I had time to go on any type of journey apart from keeping a roof over her head. Fifty hour work week sometimes. Work and her, work and her. There's been no time for me. It's always been about her.

She forgets the things I've done for her.

The school fees I've paid.

She didn't work at uni, no Saturday job

I stumped up the money

Because I wanted her to have the full university experience.

I wanted her to have what I never got to have.

But that's not good enough?

I just don't have it in me anymore to fight with her.

I'm so tired.

I just want to scream at Erica,

I'm not your superwoman

As much as I wish I was

As much as I hoped I was.

I can't do – I can't do everything...

I'm just –

> (**JOYCE** *realises she is in the middle of Stabroek Market.*)

> (*She is impressed by how beautiful it is.*)

Rarse...

I haven't smelt fruit that fresh since.... since I was little.

I'm going to have some proper food and a rum and apple juice.

Without judgement.

Stabroek Market.

And I can smell every kind of food.

Fish.

Baked goods.

Cooking oil.

Chicken.

I smell chicken.

*(**Flashback [2007]**.)*

*(**JOYCE** is sitting on the sofa looking straight ahead. The curtains are drawn, and she clearly hasn't left it for days. Takeaway pizza boxes, empty fizzy drinks bottles...)*

*(Enter **ELAINE**.)*

ELAINE. Hello, I just bringing round some chicken for all of you –

JOYCE. Mummy.

*(**ELAINE** looks around at the mess of the flat.)*

ELAINE. What happen here?

(Beat.)

Joycey. I asking you a question.

JOYCE. I'm not feeling good Mummy.

ELAINE. Where's Erica?

JOYCE. At her father's.

ELAINE. Good, so she nah haffi see yuh like this.

JOYCE. She'll be back on Sunday

ELAINE. Today is Sunday, Joyce.

JOYCE. Oh. I thought it was Friday. Time has just gotten away with me.

ELAINE. You been like this since Friday? Rotting in this room.

Why you never call me?

(Beat.)

You bathe from morning?

JOYCE. No.

ELAINE. You need to go bathe. You'll feel better once you get hot water pon yuh skin.

JOYCE. The divorce is killing me.

I'm spending all my money on lawyers, and I don't even know how I'm going to find Erica's school fees next term.

ELAINE. Yuh will find a way.

JOYCE. I don't know Mum.

It's too much.

ELAINE. Joyce, when yuh did divorce Erica's father.

It was easy?

JOYCE. No

ELAINE. But yuh get through.

JOYCE. Yeah.

ELAINE. So yuh will get through again.

God will never give you no burden, that you can't manage.

JOYCE. I was thinking Mum, that maybe I should go and see my GP.

ELAINE. You sick?

JOYCE. I think I'm depressed.

ELAINE. No Joyce, don't say that. I rebuke it in the name of the Lord.

JOYCE. I keep having these dreams. I think I'm in Guyana.

ELAINE. Yuh can't remember Guyana, you were so young when we left.

JOYCE. But I'm really small, it's like a memory. But it's not a nice feeling. It's / scary

(Sounds of broken glass. Boots on a wooden floor. Male voices.)

ELAINE. Yuh need to watch what you eat before bed, so you don't have bad dreams.

JOYCE. Everything just feels really hard.

ELAINE. So it go.

Life nah easy Joyce.

But yuh have to keep going.

JOYCE. I can't stop thinking about the / baby and –

ELAINE. No, you can't do that. You have to focus on pickney you have right now who is very much alive and will be home very soon. This is what you want her to see? Mash up house, bruk down muddah.

> *(Beat.)*

I'm going to run you a nice Dettol bath, I will scrub your back and everything. That sound good?

JOYCE. Yes Mummy.

ELAINE. I just pop round to give you lickle chicken and rice and now you got me working.

When she come back, we will have dinner together in a nice clean environment. Right?

JOYCE. Right.

ELAINE. Don't bother with no doctor in your business.

Hard times never last.

> *(The flashback fades and **JOYCE** is still holding on to her mother. We're we're back in the present day.)*

JOYCE. Everywhere, I hear her everywhere.

Mummy.

Her voice.

The rhythm.

The tone.

The cadence.

And she's in the faces of the market traders.

I hear her laughter ringing in the air.

I can feel her.

I see her.

She's everywhere.

And you know what's weird so am I?

I can see different versions of my face.

This place is full of us.

Full of we.

And it's beautiful.

It's rooted.

It's real.

And I miss her.

She did my fucking nut in that woman.

But I miss her.

(Flashback [1994].)

(Elaine's house.)

ELAINE. What yuh scared about?

JOYCE. Can I really do this? Be a good Mum?

ELAINE. You will be a good muddah Joyce. You have to mek sure you're there to protect her. Mek her know where she comes from, the lineage of women she comes from.

(Beat.)

ELAINE. A little girl! Yuh see the Obeah woman try mash up our bloodline but it never work.

You got names?

JOYCE. Not really.

ELAINE. What about Elaine?

JOYCE. Absolutely not!

ELAINE. Remember I'll be with you all di way.

JOYCE. Good, because when I've got you, I can do anything.

(**ELAINE** *embraces* **JOYCE**.)

Nine

(The Seawall.)

(**ERICA** *looks out at the water.)*

ERICA. Granny, I'm here at the seawall.

I need to talk to you.

I can see you so clearly.

(Beat.)

I just need to talk to you.

I need you.

It feels like the basic things, nurturing me, being present as my mum, holding my hands through hard shit.

It's just too much for her.

When actually, it's the bare minimum.

Why can't she do that, for me?

Am I not enough to make her want to at least try?

It feels like a cycle and I can't get out of it.

Granny, why is this so hard ?

I miss laying my head on your chest and you would tell me everything will be alright.

Ah so it go.

(Beat.)

Today I went all the way left.

I should've told her earlier about her dad but she's never there.

I hate that I let her get the best of me.

I'm working so hard to be a different version of myself.

All this rage and anger.

> *(**Flashback [2010]**.)*
>
> *(Erica's private school.)*
>
> *(Outside the headmaster's office.)*
>
> *(**ERICA** [15] sullenly sits waiting. Enter **ELAINE**.)*

Let me guess, Mum's too busy so she sent you.

ELAINE. You need to cool yuh skin, you are in big trouble.

ERICA. It's not my fault.

ELAINE. How did we get here? You weren't raised with these dutty behaviours. Back In Guyana… they would have caned me for this foolishness.

But look at this nice school, and yuh fighting like one ghetto gal?

> *(Beat.)*

ERICA. She was being bare rude about me. Saying that I'm poor.

ELAINE. So you're going to let this girl take you away from who you are?

ERICA. It's not just her though, it's this whole place. I hate it. I'm the only Black girl in my year. I don't fit in.

ELAINE. The cheque clear every term, you fit in. Whether dem like it or not.

> *(We fade into another flashback.)*
>
> *(**Flashback [2023]**.)*

(Erica's engagement party.)

*(**ERICA** is given a big bouquet of flowers. She doesn't even have to open the card.)*

ERICA. She's not coming.

ELAINE. She's been very / busy

ERICA. / It's my engagement party.

ELAINE. There will be a good reason. Open the card.

ERICA. At this point, I don't even care.

*(**ELAINE** takes the card from **ERICA** and reads it.)*

ELAINE. "Sorry not to be there darling. Have the best night. Give Lahnaray my love."

*(**ELAINE** passes **ERICA** a cheque, which is in the card as a gift.)*

ELAINE. Five hundred pounds.

ERICA. If I weren't so broke, I'd rip it up.

ELAINE. Erica. Come on, she trying.

(This memory melts into the next one.)

*(**Flashback [2007].**)*

*(Elaine's house. **ERICA** is crying and frustrated.)*

ERICA. I don't want to go to summer camp. Why can't she just look after me like a normal mum? What is wrong with her?

ELAINE. Your mother works really hard to keep a roof over your head.

ERICA. But I hated it last year, and she knows that.

ELAINE. Calm down.

> (**ERICA** *is sobbing.*)

ELAINE. What if you stay with me this summer?

ERICA. Can I please Granny? Please.

ELAINE. I'll talk to your mother.

> (**ELAINE** *pulls* **ERICA** *in for hug.*)

> (*The flashback fades out and* **ERICA** *is still holding on to* **ELAINE***'s embrace.*)

ERICA. You really were the glue that held me together.

What do you think about all this?

> (*She gestures at her stomach.*)

Mad innit.

I know there's never really a 'right' time but there's definitely a wrong time.

How did you feel when this happened to you? Were you scared?

You must have been

You did it by yourself.

And so did Mum – pretty much.

This would change everything

Let's not even get into pushing a whole human out your –

Yeah. I dunno.

Maybe you're both just stronger than I am.

Rah, I don't know how you did it all – I think about that a lot.

Especially, after seeing that sickness take over your body and mind

The strong, proud woman who held everything just went.

You were so small and frail

You weighed nothing

I tried to hold on to what was little was left of you at the end

Sometimes you looked straight through me...

Please tell me you knew I was there.

I held you in my arms as you took your final breath.

I breathed with you until you stopped.

> *(Beat.)*

It's Thursday. 16th June. Your anniversary. Maybe that's why I can feel you even stronger right now. Right here.

But it's like the closer I am to you, the further away I feel from mum.

Maybe it's always been like that?

I just wish I could hear your voice.

> *(**Flashback [2022]**.)*

> *(Elaine's house. **ELAINE** embraces **ERICA** [27].)*

ELAINE. I have to go back Erica.

I have to go back home to Guyana.

ERICA. We'll do it then, me and you.

ELAINE. And your mother. She is coming with us.

ERICA. Is she?

ELAINE. How you mean? Of course.

Me and my girls are going home.

> *(Beat.)*

Erica, you need to find a way with your mother.

Too much mix up with the two of you.

ERICA. It's not all down to me.

ELAINE. Promise me Erica.

Promise me, you'll find a way. And that we will all go Guyana.

ERICA. I promise.

> *(Her phone rings. It's Lanre.)*

This guy's timing…

> *(She looks down at her phone and then sees the time.)*

Fuck! It's nearly one p.m. I gotta get over to Ranjani's.

Ten

(Outside hotel.)

(**ERICA** *is waiting for her taxi to pick her up. She checks the time. No sign of Joyce. She gets in the cab. Central Cee's "Sprinter" plays.* *A moment as she waits.)*

ERICA. Clive, let's just go.

(**JOYCE** *opens the door and is in the car.)*

JOYCE. What a tune!

Central Cee.

I'm so glad I caught you in time. I need to talk to you.

Clive, can you turn down the music?

(Clive turns the music down.)

I saw Mummy. I saw her. She came to me.

Erica this place, I never thought I had a connection here but I get it now.

ERICA. What do you get?

JOYCE. I get what you've been going on about. The ancestors, our connection –

ERICA. What exactly did I say?

JOYCE. Don't do that – this is difficult for me –

ERICA. Difficult for you?

JOYCE. I'm trying to explain –

ERICA. Are you? Are you really, yeah?

---

* A licence to produce *Not Your Superwoman* does not include a performance licence for any third-party or copyrighted recordings. Licensees should create their own.

JOYCE. I saw her – she came back to me –

ERICA. Well, she's never left me.

> *(Beat.)*

All of this, all I have tried to do is be here, with you –
for us to discover our family, your father, together – be
HERE with / her –

JOYCE. / Erica. Stop. What you did was a violation –

ERICA. How? By telling you the truth?

JOYCE. It hurt me.

ERICA. I know it was a lot, I'm sorry – but do you really
think it is my intention to hurt you?

JOYCE. I don't want to talk about –

ERICA. You can't keep doing that. We have to talk about it!

JOYCE. You have no idea what I've been through / babe

ERICA. / BECAUSE YOU DON'T TALK TO ME! You
don't communicate.

This is chaos. I just wanted everything to go to plan
today, take Granny home to Ranjani's /

JOYCE. / Ranjani's? Oh shit, it's the anniversary – supposed
to be there at three.

ERICA. Yeah, again. You always do this Mum.

This whole trip was supposed to be healing for us. But
there's never really been an 'us' has there?

You haven't been present. It's a cycle that's eating us up.

> *(Beat. **ERICA** remembers her techniques and*
> *continues.)*

You make me feel unwanted. You were always trying to
replace me with something – your man Sean, your job,
another holiday, another baby –

JOYCE. Erica... be careful with what you're saying.

> (**ERICA** *isn't listening, and is getting it all out.*)

ERICA. No I'm gonna say it, and you're gonna listen.

You didn't even turn up to my engagement party – and I know I'm a big big woman but it still hurts –

You want to be superwoman and handle everything on your own. And you expect me to do it all alone too. And I can't.

You left me to look after Granny by myself. She literally died in my arms and you weren't there. Isn't it mad that we've never spoken about that?

> (**JOYCE** *avoids her gaze, ashamed.*)

This shit is only going to stop if you're willing to do the work mum. You can mock my therapy all you like but you've got to do the work.

I just want to be Sabrina. I just want you to see me, to hear me, to understand me.

We have to understand each other.

> (*Beat.*)

Mum? Are you listening?

> (**JOYCE** *doesn't respond and they carry on in silence.*)
>
> (*Silence.*)

JOYCE. We're here.

Eleven

(**ERICA** *jumps out of the car and begins steamrolling towards Ranjani's. Ranjani is a now a broken down building that has fallen in on itself.* **JOYCE** *gets out the car and follows her daughter.*)

(*She begins walking and then freezes when she sees the building.*)

(**ERICA** *looks at her mother.*)

JOYCE. Do you hear that?

(*Sounds of footsteps.* **JOYCE** *is going into herself.*)

ERICA. Hear what?

JOYCE. I've always had these dreams.

Well more like nightmares to be honest

And I never really understood them.

Images.

Feelings.

Smells.

We were playing in the store.

Hide and seek, eye spy.

And then she locks up and I'm round the back, waiting for her.

And they came.

Men.

Men in balaclavas with guns.

I remember they took Mummy into the backroom.

I could hear her.

>(**JOYCE** *fades into the flashback.* **ERICA** *reacts through all of this.*)

>(***Flashback [1973] Ranjani's.***)

>(**JOYCE** *[4] is watching* **ELAINE** *[21] on the floor crying.*)

Mummy. Please don't cry.

Mummy.

>(*She hugs* **ELAINE**. **ELAINE** *leans into* **JOYCE** *and cries harder. The next section plays in and out of the present and the past.* **ERICA** *and* **ELAINE** *are alive in this space.*)

There's a pit in my stomach.

And a pinched feeling.

I close my eyes and wait.

I want my Mum.

I want my Mum.

They left eventually and we.

Just sat there for hours.

>(*Beat.*)

We were girls.

Black girls.

Unprotected Black girls.

And then we left.

We came to England.

(**JOYCE** *is piecing things together live.*)

JOYCE. She was protecting me...! She spent her whole life protecting me.

(***Flashback [1976] London.***)

(*Same positioning as before, but this time* **ELAINE** *[24] is not crying. She is stoic.* **JOYCE** *[8] stands behind her mother, with the same facial expression. She puts her hand on her shoulder.*)

(*In the present and in the past at the same time...*)

(*Silence.*)

ERICA. Do you want to leave mum?

(*Beat.*)

JOYCE. You know I never saw her cry. After that one time. Never again.

(**JOYCE** *begins to cry.* **ERICA** *holds her.* **ERICA** *begins to cry too.*)

JOYCE. I'm not OK.

ERICA. Nor am I.

JOYCE. I am so sorry I made you feel unwanted. You were always wanted.

(***Flashback [2005].***)

Hey Babe.

(*Beat.*)

Are you not talking to me anymore?

(**ERICA** *stops tapping and looks to* **JOYCE**.)

ERICA. No.

JOYCE. I'm sorry babe, I'm late picking you up again.

I've had a bit of a hard time.

But it's no excuse I'm going to do better.

I'm going to be better.

ERICA. Are you getting divorced, again?

JOYCE. That's big people business Erica.

> *(Beat.)*

Probably.

> *(Beat.)*

Can I have a cuddle?

> (**ERICA** *cuddles up to* **JOYCE**.*)*

What you watching?

> (**ERICA** *flicks through the channels, comes across VH1 and Leann Rimes' "How Do I Live" plays.**)

I love this song.

> (**JOYCE** *and* **ERICA** *sing along.)*

It's gonna be just the two us for a little bit babe, that's alright isn't it?

ERICA. Yeah.

JOYCE. That's good, because when I'm with you I can do anything.

> *(The flashback fades and we are back in the present day.)*

---

* A licence to produce *Not Your Superwoman* does not include a performance licence for any third-party or copyrighted recordings. Licensees should create their own.

ERICA. Let's get out of here. We shouldn't scatter granny here.

JOYCE. No wait, wait. We need to be here. We need to do this together. We need to find an understanding of what happened here, what happened to granny, to us, to you. I want to reclaim this space Erica. For our family. For the women in our family.

> (**JOYCE** *grabs a small bottle of rum from* **ERICA**. *She pours libation.*)

Thank you Mummy for mothering us.

ERICA. Thank you Granny.

> (**JOYCE** *grabs* **ERICA**.)

JOYCE. Mummy. I want to thank you for all of your struggles. Thank you for coming to see me.

For making me see you. This land, our land, for making me see my daughter.

I wish we had spoken about what we went through here.

But I think I get it.

I get why we didn't, I get why we had to struggle.

You had to protect me. And it was hard for both of us.

You always told me.

That no one is going to save me.

No man is going to lift me up and out of this.

This womanhood.

This blackness.

This struggle.

This pain.

So you got to find your own light.

And I did.

Erica you are my light, I am guided by my daughter, who faces the world head on. Like a proper bad gyal.

(*She turns to* **ERICA**.)

JOYCE. No more assumptions... I will talk to you, but you have to talk to me. No secrets.

ERICA. Well, it's that or we call an Obeah woman to end the curse on the family.

JOYCE. You really are Mummy 2.0 aren't you? Read the room

ERICA. (*Laughing.*) I couldn't resist.

(*Beat.*)

Think about it – when you're ready, just pass through.

(*Beat.*)

It couldn't have been easy for you.

Holding everything the way you did.

And I really do appreciate the sacrifices you made for me. But I needed you.

JOYCE. I can see that now, I'm sorry I pushed you away.

ERICA. It's cool.

JOYCE. I'm even sorry about bloody summer camp.

ERICA. Yeah, you're foul for that. Summer Camp was the worst. The orchestra one. Hell.

JOYCE. I thought it would be enriching.

ERICA. It wasn't.

(**JOYCE** *and* **ERICA** *laugh.*)

(*Beat.*)

JOYCE. I got no excuse for Mummy. I should have been there babe. I tried to get there, I really did.

I wish she'd held on, but she'd held on enough.

> *(Beat.)*

ERICA. How are you, mum?

JOYCE. That's the first time someone has asked me that in years.

I don't know.

> *(Beat.)*

I'm here. I'm standing. How are you, Erica?

ERICA. I'm trying to accept what I can't control. As granny would say, so it go.

> *(Beat.)*

JOYCE. You are my bones.

My blood.

My sweat.

My life.

> *(Both **ELAINE** and **JOYCE** say the following as they morph into flashback, the embrace / arm in shoulder.)*

JOYCE/ELAINE. I armed you.

I gave you all the tools I could.

I love you so much.

This is real love.

It's heart and guts.

It's sacrifice

And it's hard

And it hurts

(Goes back to just **JOYCE**.*)*

JOYCE. But you are more than equipped, my girl.

You are more than equipped.

ERICA. Sorry, equipped for what?

JOYCE. Being a mother.

ERICA. When did you decide what I was doing?

JOYCE. Well the way you were talking –

ERICA. When did you hear me say anything?

I found out I was pregnant three days ago, literally chill.

JOYCE. Well, with all this spiritual shit – I just thought –

ERICA. This is what you do, you get an idea, and you run with it.

Do you ever listen?

JOYCE. You do talk a lot babe.

ERICA. Wooooow. I talk a lot?

JOYCE. I do think I'll be a good Grandmother, well Glam mother?

ERICA. Glam mother? What even is that?

JOYCE. Baby or not, I'm there for you.

But if you're thinking names what, about Joyce?

ERICA. No, just. No.

(BLACKOUT.)

9 780573 000898